The Perfect Party

The perfect party

Written by Christine Peymani

Bath · New York · Singapore · Hong Kong · Cologne · Delhi · Melbourne

First published by Parragon in 2008
Parragon
Queen Street House
4 Queen Street
Bath BA1 1HE, UK

ISBN 978-1-4075-2502-0

Printed in UK

Chapter 1

"I am *so* ready for Hawaii," Jade announced to her best friends on the last day before summer break. "I mean, check me out!" She plucked a flower from the vase on her mum's kitchen counter and tucked it behind her ear, then struck a hula pose, arms wafting out to the side, mimicking the gentle movement of the ocean's waves with a serene smile on her face.

"You'll definitely fit right in," her best friend, Cloe, agreed.

"Right, because everyone in Hawaii spends all their time doing the hula," Sasha teased, winking at her best friends.

"What, don't they?" Grinning, Jade kept dancing, swaying from side to side as she hummed a few bars of "Aloha 'Oe," a pretty

Hawaiian song she had learned as soon as she found out they were going to Hawaii.

"I guess we'll find out soon," Yasmin pointed out. The four best friends had applied to do a cultural exchange programme in Hawaii right after school finished, and they were thrilled that they had all been accepted. During their time in Hawaii, they would get to learn about traditional Hawaiian arts like hula, ukulele, and lei-making, and they couldn't wait!

"Are you girls all packed?" Jade's mum swept into the kitchen and surveyed the girls perched at her kitchen counter.

Jade stopped dancing and nodded emphatically. "Of course we are!" She was so excited for this trip that she had packed everything days in advance instead of agonizing over her outfit options until the very last minute like she usually would. She just knew her fresh sense of style would fit in perfectly on the lush Hawaiian islands.

"Well then, we'd better get you to the airport." The girls followed Jade's mum outside, hoisting their tote bags onto their shoulders and dragging their rolling suitcases behind them. They piled into the car and Jade's mum drove them to their airport, where the rest of their parents met them at check-in.

"I'm so glad we didn't miss seeing you off!" Sasha's mum cried, wrapping her daughter in a big hug, though she pulled away quickly when her BlackBerry buzzed, and she began rapidly typing out a message.

©MGA

"Come on, girls, we'd better get moving," interrupted Miss Lang, their social studies teacher and the leader of the trip, ushering her students towards the security line. The girls hugged their parents goodbye, then hurried after their teacher, chattering excitedly with each other.

On the plane, Yasmin and Cloe sat together, with Sasha and Jade behind them. The girls all settled in for a long flight. Yasmin pulled out her eBook reader, Cloe listened to her iPod, Sasha popped in a movie on her portable DVD player and Jade grabbed a fashion magazine.

But soon Cloe got tired of listening to her music and turned to Yasmin, eager to talk. "What do you want to do first when we land?" she asked.

"Hmm?" Yasmin murmured, her eyes glued to her book.

"Yas, are you listening to me?" Cloe waved her hands impatiently in front of her friend's face to catch her attention.

"Hang on, just let me finish this page." Yasmin didn't even glance up, and Cloe slumped back into her seat with a dramatic sigh. After a moment, Yasmin turned off the screen of her eBook reader and turned to her friend. "What's up, Clo?"

"I'm *bored*," Cloe complained. "This flight goes on, like, *forever.*"

"Don't you have your guidebook with you? Why don't you check that out?" Yasmin suggested helpfully.

"Because I'm sure you've memorized it already," Cloe replied. Yasmin just smiled — she *had* pretty much absorbed the whole book as soon as they learned they would be going on this trip.

"You're supposed to be learning about Hawaiian culture too, you know," Yasmin pointed out.

"I will – I'm just more of a hands-on type of person, you know?" Cloe explained.

"Well, we'll definitely be getting plenty of hands-on exposure to Hawaiian culture," Yasmin agreed. "But in the meantime, why don't you take a nap or something? It'll make the time go faster."

Yasmin turned back to her book, and Cloe sighed, feeling abandoned. She stared out of the window at the plump clouds skittering past, and finally she drifted off, her head propped against her little pink travel pillow.

The next thing she knew, Yasmin was shaking her awake. "We're here, sleepyhead!" Yasmin declared, and Cloe's eyes fluttered open at the sound of her friend's voice.

"We're in Hawaii already?" she murmured sleepily, and Yasmin laughed.

"Weren't you the one who was just complaining that this flight was too long?" Yasmin asked as she grabbed her tote from under the seat in front of her.

"I guess sleeping did make it go by faster," Cloe admitted. She stretched her arms over her head and yawned, still rousing herself from her nap and trying to feel awake.

"Are you girls ready to soak up some tropical paradise?" Jade asked, slipping into the aisle behind them.

"Always!" Cloe agreed, perking up.

"I'm glad you're excited, girls, but remember, you're here to learn," Miss Lang reminded them, shuffling along behind her eager students.

"Don't worry, we can't *wait* to learn all

7

about Hawaiian culture," Sasha assured their teacher with a smile.

When the girls stepped past security, they were immediately greeted by a cluster of girls about their own age holding up a sign reading "Welcome, Stilesville Students" in big, sparkly green letters.

"Aloha, and welcome to Hawaii!" one of the girls exclaimed, stepping forward and draping a purple orchid lei around Yasmin's neck. Her classmates did the same for each of the other three girls and their teacher.

"I could get used to this," Jade murmured, and her friends nodded in agreement.

"I'm Lani," the first girl said, holding out her hand, "and these are my friends Alana, Kaila and Mya." Alana gave them a warm smile, Kaila a shy little wave, and Mya a brisk nod of acknowledgement.

"We'll be helping you learn all about Hawaii," Alana told them eagerly.

"And I'm their teacher, Ms Sato," added the woman next to them, her hair tucked neatly into a bun. She held out her hand to their teacher. "You must be Miss Lang."

While the teachers began discussing lesson plans for the next two weeks, the eight girls looked at each other uncertainly.

After a moment, Lani broke the silence again. "We are *so* excited to have you girls here to learn all about our beautiful island."

"We're totally ready to tap into the island culture," Yasmin agreed.

Lani gave her a wide smile. "*So* glad to hear it, I'm sure you'll love it here."

They followed their teachers outside and piled into a big blue van that was waiting for them in the garage. "You'll be staying at one of

my favourite local hotels," Lani informed them. "I'm totally jealous that we don't get to stay there with you."

"I'm sure we could arrange for a sleepover, if you want," Cloe suggested with a grin.

"A sleepover!" Lani exchanged amused glances with Mya, who hid a snicker behind her hand. "I haven't had a sleepover in *years*! That sounds just *adorable*!"

Now Cloe and her friends looked at each other, wondering how much fun it was actually going to be to spend the next few weeks with these girls.

"Well, we do like to think of ourselves as adorable," Jade said finally, and her friends all laughed. After a moment, the other girls joined in, and Jade and her friends hoped that maybe these girls were okay after all.

Chapter 2

The four best friends felt like they had just fallen asleep in the room they were all sharing when there was a brisk knock on their door.

"Time for your first hula class!" Lani called out cheerfully.

Although they were seriously jetlagged, the girls rushed to get all freshened up and ready to tackle their first lesson in Hawaiian culture. They all decided to dress up for their first hula lesson in their cutest island attire. Cloe wore a pink strapless sundress, Jade a polka-dot print shift, Sasha an orange flowerprint halter dress, and Yasmin a brightly patterned dress with billowy sleeves which she'd bought for the trip.

In cut-off shorts and a tank top, Lani looked way more casual. She raised her eyebrows

at the girls' outfits. "You know hula's a serious workout, right? Are you sure you'll be comfortable in those fancy threads?"

Jade exchanged glances with her friends before announcing, "Oh, we're always comfortable with looking good!"

Lani raised her eyebrows. "Okay then. We'd better get going. Mrs Kauwe hates to be kept waiting."

The girls scurried after Lani, anxious not to be late for their very first class on the cultural exchange.

The dance studio looked a lot like the one where the girls

took hip-hop classes back home, with parquet floors and mirrors lining the walls. Alana, Kaila and Mya were already there, lined up in front of a woman with long black hair who was dressed in a pretty hibiscus-print dress.

"We're thrilled to have you girls here with us," Mrs Kauwe announced. "These are some of my best students, so they'll be happy to help you learn the moves."

Cloe, Jade, Sasha and Yasmin joined the other girls in front of the mirrored wall.

"Now, have any of you ever tried hula before?" their dance teacher asked.

Jade raised her hand. "I've done some research and I know a few steps."

Mya smirked. "I'm sure you do."

Mrs Kauwe shot the tall, willowy girl a warning look. "Great, let's see what you know," she told Jade.

Jade repeated the swaying steps she had done back home in her own kitchen, and her teacher smiled approvingly.

"That's an excellent start," Mrs Kauwe announced. "That's called the ka'o step, or sway step. Now why don't we all try it together, on the count of three?"

She led the eight girls in three basic hula steps, the kaholo, ka'o and ami, then helped them add in hand motions as well. Alana led the others in helping the newcomers get the steps and arm positions right, beautifully demonstrating each step for them. Soon they were all swaying in unison to the soothing strains of the traditional Hawaiian music wafting from Mrs Kauwe's CD player.

"You're really getting it!" their teacher exclaimed after they had run through the moves several times. "That's all we have time for today, but next time we'll start learning the routine that

we'll perform at our final recital at the end of next week."

"We're learning a whole routine in two weeks?" Sasha cried. She was used to learning dance routines fast, but two weeks was almost no time at all!

"What's wrong?" Mya asked. "Don't you think you can keep up?"

"Oh, I can do more than keep up," Sasha declared back. "Give me a couple days and I'll be choreographing my own hula routines."

"Seriously, Sasha's an amazing choreographer," Cloe chimed in.

Mya and Lani looked sceptical, but Mrs Kauwe said, "I'd love to feature an original dance if you really think you can put it together in time."

Although she wasn't sure that she actually could, having never done a single step of hula before that day, Sasha was never one to back down from a challenge. "No problem."

As the girls left the studio, Yasmin leaned in and whispered to Sasha, "How are you going to make up a new routine in a new dance style in a couple of days?"

Sasha shrugged. "I'll figure something out."

"You always do!" Jade agreed, making Sasha smile. With her best friends there to help her, Sasha was sure she would find some way to pull it off. After all, she always had enjoyed a challenge.

Next the girls had their first ukulele lesson. Since they all played guitar, they figured this instrument, which looked like a miniature guitar, would be easy. But once they were settled into the music room with their ukuleles cradled in their arms, they soon realized that to get the

sound right, they would have to do everything differently.

"I can tell that you girls are very musical," Miss Akana, their ukulele instructor, declared as soon as they had strummed a few notes.

"We are, aren't we?" Cloe said, flipping her hair back over her shoulders and looking pleased.

"If you call that music," Mya muttered. She and her friends were supposed to be helping the girls with their ukulele lessons as well, but so far they hadn't been very helpful at all.

Ignoring her, Jade announced, "This is such a cool instrument! I can totally see us using it in some of our band's songs."

"Oh, yeah, I'm already thinking up some new uke-inspired tunes!" Yasmin cried.

"They sing, they dance — is there anything they can't do?" Lani asked, shooting a glance at Mya.

"Not that I can think of," Jade replied.

"So are you going to whip up some new songs by next week too?" Mya demanded.

Before Yasmin could stop her, Sasha declared, "Sure, why not? Yasmin's an incredible songwriter — she'll be writing for the uke in no time, trust me."

"I wish I could do that," Alana murmured, but Mya silenced her with a piercing glare.

"That's enough, ladies," Miss Akana interrupted. "Right now we need to practise

our scales. Do you think you can manage that?"

Her students all nodded obediently and followed her lead in strumming a few more chords. The girls were impressed by the especially sonorous sounds coming from Kaila's instrument as she played gently.

"Good job, everyone," their teacher said. "Tomorrow we'll start learning a song so we'll be all ready for our concert next week!"

The girls packed up their ukuleles, and although they were excited about all the new things they were learning, they couldn't help feeling nervous about how much they had to accomplish in the next two weeks. It looked like they wouldn't have any time to relax at all on this island vacation!

Chapter 3

That night, Cloe lay awake even after all her friends had drifted off to sleep. Although she was exhausted from all the day's activities, she couldn't seem to get to sleep. What kept her up was the fear that, in all the excitement of their trip, her friends had completely forgotten all about her birthday.

When she first realized that her birthday would fall on the last Saturday of their trip, she was totally pumped — after all, what could be cooler than a birthday celebration in Hawaii? She hadn't even mentioned it to her best friends, because of course they would remember her birthday, and plan something fabulous like they always did.

But now that they were here and none

of her friends had said a word about her birthday, Cloe was getting worried. She stared at the ceiling, restraining herself from shaking her friends awake to demand to know how they could have forgotten all about her big day; after all, they were her best friends!

With a sigh, she slipped out of bed and crept out onto their room's balcony, careful not to disturb her sleeping friends. Outside, the ocean breeze brushed her face and fluttered through her hair, and she closed her eyes, soaking in the night air. She listened to the waves lapping gently on the sand below, and gazed up at the bright stars in the clear sky above her.

She reminded herself that even if she didn't have a party, this was still a spectacular place to kick off the next year of her life. But Cloe loved celebrating her birthday, and hard as she tried, she couldn't quite convince herself that just being here was celebration enough.

Shivering as a strong gust of wind swept over her, she headed back inside. She climbed back into bed and finally drifted off to sleep, dreaming of balloons, cakes, piles of presents and her best friends celebrating her.

"Operation Birthday Luau is officially under way," Yasmin told Jade and Sasha the next morning while Cloe was in the shower. "I talked to Miss Akana after class, and she's handling the music."

"And Mrs Kauwe will arrange for the entertainment," Sasha added.

"Great!" Jade perched on the edge of her bed, leaning towards her friends eagerly. "And we have our Hawaiian cooking class today, so hopefully we'll get some fabulous menu ideas to make sure everything is totally yummy."

"I was hoping that some of our fellow students could help us with the planning, but somehow I don't think those girls would be interested." Yasmin flopped on the other bed, a frustrated expression on her face.

"Well, Lani and Mya wouldn't," Sasha admitted. "But I think Kaila and Alana just might, they seem much friendlier."

"Those two do seem sweet," Jade agreed. "I'd definitely like to get to know them better."

"It would be a huge help if we could get some local perspective on planning this party," Yasmin said. "So I hope you girls are right!"

"We'll be with all four girls all day again today," Sasha pointed out, "so we'll have plenty of time to get a sense of who might be willing to pitch in."

"I'm sure we can bring them around with the force of our charm," Jade replied with a

grin. "Girls, get ready to make some new friends!"

Just then, Cloe emerged from the bathroom in a pair of cute brown capris and a fluttery sage-green top, still towelling off her long blonde hair.

"Who are we making friends with?" she asked.

"Oh, the other girls in our class, hopefully," Yasmin told her hurriedly. She couldn't believe they had almost let Cloe overhear their plans for her surprise party!

"Really?" Cloe paused her vigorous towel drying to shoot her friends a surprised look. "They didn't seem too friendly."

"Yeah, well, you never know who might make a great new friend," Jade chimed in.

"I guess ..." Cloe shrugged, not seeming at all convinced, but turned her attention back to

her hair without asking anything more.

Her best friends looked at each other in relief, and Yasmin hopped off the bed, announcing, "I've got the next shower!" She figured they had better get moving – they had another big day ahead of them!

"So what made you decide to help out with this programme?" Yasmin asked Kaila in their first lesson of the day, a cooking class. Their teacher, Mr Jones, had paired each of the visiting girls with a local girl to help them learn how to properly prepare Hawaiian cuisine, and Yasmin was relieved she had got Kaila as her partner.

She glanced over at Cloe at the next table, who actually seemed to be having a good time with Lani – the two of them were already laughing hysterically at something.

Jade and Alana also seemed to be hitting it off. Meanwhile, Sasha sat silently examining the recipe their instructor had given them, not exchanging a single word with her partner Mya, who was staring in the other direction.

"Oh, I just love our Hawaiian culture," Kaila replied in a soft voice, "and I thought it would be so much fun to share it with students from the mainland as Hawaii is such a special place."

"Well, I'm glad you did." Yasmin met the girl's big brown eyes and gave her a friendly smile, though Kaila quickly looked away. Yasmin shook her head – she was shy herself, but this girl gave the word a whole new twist!

©MGA

"I hope it isn't too boring for you, going through all these classes with us for stuff you already know how to do," Yasmin continued, still hoping to draw the other girl out.

"Oh, no, there's always something new to learn about all of these arts," Kaila assured her.

"That's how I feel about my favourite classes back home," Yasmin agreed. "I mean, sometimes I'll sit in on a creative writing workshop or yoga class or voice lesson, and I always feel like I get something out of it, especially as I put a lot into them, too."

"Are those the things you usually do back home?" Kaila asked, her eyes bright with curiosity and wonder.

"Oh, yeah, I love to write, and yoga totally soothes me *and* keeps me in shape, and of course I have to keep my voice in shape for the band I sing in with my best friends," Yasmin explained at length.

"That all sounds really cool," Kaila murmured, looking down at the recipe in front of them.

"You know, I could give you a lesson in any of those things, if you're interested," Yasmin told her. "I mean, this is supposed to be a cultural exchange programme, so you ought to get something out of the deal too!"

"Oh, I don't know …" Kaila let her dark veil of curls fall over her face, looking embarrassed. "There's so much for you all to do while you're here. I wouldn't want to take up too much of your time."

"There's always time to share my favourite activities with my friends!" Yasmin insisted, but before she could say anything else, Mr Jones waved his hands to get the class's attention.

"Okay, who's ready to cook?" he asked. The girls all smiled at him, but he cupped his hand to his ear and cried, "I can't hear you!"

They all exclaimed, "I am!" and he grinned, looking at the class in front of him.

"All right, then!" Looking pleased, he held up a small, purple, potato-like object. "Let's start with taro, the staple food of the Hawaiian diet and the basis of many traditional recipes."

"Why's it purple?" Cloe asked, staring at the bowlful of taro in front of her uncertainly.

"Why are sweet potatoes orange, or butternut squashes yellow?" Mr Jones replied. "It's all just part of nature's amazing variety!"

"Okay ..." But Cloe continued to poke at the taro with her fork, not convinced that this would be a tasty item.

Lani leaned over and whispered, "It's good, seriously. You'll be pleasantly surprised."

"You're probably just used to it," Cloe told her, and Lani laughed.

"Well then, I guess you'll just have to get

used to it, too!" Lani scooted her chair closer to Cloe's and started organizing the ingredients and mixing bowls arrayed on the table in front of them.

"Come on, girls, let's get cooking!" Mr Jones interrupted, and he began leading them through the process of baking taro rolls, which came out purple like the vegetable they were made from – and tasted absolutely delicious!

"Mmm, why don't we have this back home?" Cloe asked through a mouthful of roll.

"I told you you'd like it!" Lani replied, giggling at Cloe's enthusiasm as Cloe's friends watched, suspicious at Lani's sudden friendliness. Mya, too, looked annoyed that her friend seemed to have decided the new girls were worth being nice to after all.

"Keep an eye on her," Alana whispered to Jade, glancing around to make sure no one else overheard.

"Seriously?" Jade asked, her green eyes wide with surprise. She didn't trust Lani, but Alana sounded so serious that she had to wonder if there was something more going on here than met the eye.

Alana's eyes darted over to Lani, then back to Jade. "I'll explain later. Maybe we can meet up for lunch after this?"

"Sure," Jade agreed. Now she had to know more! "Can my friends come too?"

"Oh, of course," Alana replied, and suddenly her friendly smile was back. "You girls are all so nice!"

"Well, thanks," Jade said. As they cleaned up the spray of flour that dusted their worktable, she struggled to contain her curiosity, reminding herself that her new friend would explain everything soon enough.

Chapter 4

"Do you girls wanna grab some lunch?" Cloe asked her best friends as they headed out of the classroom and into the dazzling Hawaiian sun, feeling it warm them with its rays.

Her friends exchanged looks, unsure what to say. They wanted to get the scoop on Lani, and since Cloe seemed to be making friends with her, they weren't sure she would like what Alana had to say.

"Actually, I was hoping to get Kaila's help on ukulele over lunch," Yasmin said. "I really need to get started on my new song!"

"And Alana is supposed to help me with some hula moves," Sasha added. "They've got us so booked up here that I need every spare second to work on my routine."

"What about you, Jade?" Cloe asked, her eyes bright with hope.

"I might just go and lie down for a little bit," Jade replied. "Absorbing all this culture is totally wearing me out!"

"Oh." Cloe murmured, looking disappointed and a little crestfallen.

But just then, Lani and Mya appeared beside her. "Why don't you come to lunch with us?" Lani suggested. "There's an awesome café right next door that I'm sure you'd love."

Cloe immediately perked up. "Sounds great!" She hurried off, giggling with the two other girls without giving her best friends another glance.

"My house is right near here," Alana told them once Cloe and the others were out of earshot. "Why don't we go and talk there?"

33

At Alana's house, the girls pulled up stools at her kitchen counter while she made them kahlua pork sandwiches.

"Lani, Mya, Kaila and I became best friends when we started taking hula lessons together when we were three," Alana began as she handed each girl a sandwich. "We were inseparable, just like you girls."

"So what happened?" Yasmin asked, leaning across the counter.

"By the time we started high school, Lani and Mya were more into being cool than hanging out with their old friends," Kaila explained in her whispery voice.

"But you girls are cool!" Jade protested.

"Thanks," Kaila replied, blushing.

"But Lani and Mya don't agree," Alana added. "Once they became cheerleading co-captains, they wanted to spend all their time

on that – not boring stuff like the traditional Hawaiian classes we love."

"Then why are they part of this exchange programme?" Sasha wanted to know.

"Because it'll look good on their college applications," Alana explained.

"Plus their parents really want them to stay in these classes, so they have to," Kaila said.

"So you girls aren't friends anymore?" Yasmin asked.

"Not really," Alana admitted. "We put up with each other, but we haven't been close in years, not like we used to be."

"They just aren't very nice anymore," Kaila murmured. "It's sad."

"So why are they being so nice to Cloe?" Yasmin inquired.

"I'm not exactly sure," Alana replied, settling onto a stool beside the other girls.

"She's seemed a little upset since you guys got here, so maybe Lani just figured she would be the easiest target."

"They're obsessed with everything and everyone from the mainland lately," Kaila added. "They keep saying how they can't wait to get off the island."

Gazing out of the window at the lush tropical plants and vibrant flowers that crowded Alana's garden, Jade shook her head in disbelief. "Why would anyone ever want to leave here?"

Their new friends shrugged. "It doesn't make any sense to us, either," Alana said.

"Back up a second," Sasha interrupted, pushing her empty plate away from her. "You guys think Cloe seems upset?"

Alana and Kaila turned to look at each other, then nodded slowly.

"I bet she thinks we aren't doing anything for her birthday," Yasmin declared.

"That *is* the danger of a surprise party," Jade pointed out.

"When's her birthday?" Alana paused in the process of gathering up the girls' plates and piling them in the sink and turned to the girls who were lined up at the counter.

"It's a week from Saturday," Sasha replied. "We're planning to throw her a luau, and we were actually hoping you two might be willing to help out."

"Absolutely!" Alana agreed excitedly. "We *love* planning luaus!"

"Oh my gosh, really?" Yasmin squealed. "We've never even been to a luau, so we have no clue what we're doing."

"And we *have* to throw Cloe the best party ever," Jade added.

"Yeah, especially since she thinks we aren't doing anything at all," Sasha chimed in.

"Mrs Kauwe and Miss Akana have already agreed to help out," Yasmin told them.

"Oh, and I just talked to Mr Jones, and he's handling the food," Jade announced.

"Wow, you're off to a great start!" Alana cried. "Are you sure you need our help?"

"If we're gonna pull the whole thing together in less than two weeks, then we sure do!" Sasha insisted. She glanced at her watch and gasped. "Uh-oh, we're supposed to be at our lei-making class, like, now. Let's go, girls!"

She took a final gulp of the passion fruit, orange and guava juice Alana had given her and rushed out through the door after her friends, feeling better already about everything they had to do in the next couple of weeks.

"Leis are one of the most beautiful Hawaiian traditions," declared Ms Silva, their arts and crafts teacher. "They are a symbol of love, respect and welcome that embody the spirit of aloha."

All eight girls sat around a big table piled with gorgeous purple orchids. Cloe picked up a blossom and gazed at it admiringly. "I'm all for any tradition that involves fabulous accessories!"

"We'll be trying the kui method today," Ms Silva explained. "Pluck off the stems, then take a length of string and thread about 50 flowers right through the middle. Once you have a nice full string of flowers, grab a colourful ribbon and tie off the end."

As they all began threading their leis, Jade asked Cloe, "So, did you girls have a nice lunch at the cafe?"

"We sure did," Lani replied before Cloe could say a word. "Too bad you all couldn't join us."

"Guess you really needed that extra practice though, huh?" Mya asked, smirking.

"Well, practice makes perfect, and I always aim for perfection." Sasha didn't even raise her eyes from the delicate blossom she was gently guiding onto her thread.

"I wish you could've hung out with us

though," Cloe interrupted, looking anxiously from her best friends to her new friends.

"Next time," Yasmin promised.

"Oh good, something to look forward to," Lani replied, her voice brassy with false enthusiasm and barely-disguised dislike.

"How are those leis coming?" Ms Silva clapped her hands together to get her students' attention, and they each held up their strands of flowers for her approval. "Lovely, ladies! And when you're finished, you can all exchange them with each other!"

Jade, Sasha and Yasmin glanced at each other, all thinking the same thing – there was no way they would be offering leis to Lani or Mya, who were bound to criticize their handiwork. They all felt bad about it, but none of them were feeling exactly warm towards either of those girls.

Chapter 5

The next morning dawned sunny and clear, and the girls couldn't have been more thrilled. They would be taking their first surfing lesson that morning, which would be their first chance to hit the beach since their arrival in Hawaii.

"Did you know that surfing was invented by Hawaiian royalty?" Yasmin asked, and her friends grinned at her.

"I *knew* you memorized that guidebook!" Cloe teased, but Yasmin just shrugged.

"What? It was interesting." She walked along the beach a little ahead of her friends, her flip-flops slapping against the sand.

"It's so cool that surfing is a central part of

Hawaiian culture," Jade agreed.

"What can I say?" Sasha replied. "Hawaii's a cool place!"

In their flower-print and striped one-piece swimsuits, the four best friends strolled along the edge of the ocean on Waikiki Beach, waiting for their surfing instructor.

"There they are!" Lani shouted from down the beach, running towards them. "We were supposed to meet over there!" She pointed further down the sand, where her friends and a tall young man, all carrying surfboards, stood waiting.

"Sorry – guess we had trouble recognizing the right dune of sand," Sasha said, annoyed.

Cloe glared at her friend before turning to Lani. "Thanks for coming to get us." She hurried after Lani while her friends trailed behind, looking at each other in confusion.

"Hi, I'm Kai, and I'll be your surfing teacher," said the tanned young man who stood with the girls' Hawaiian hosts.

"Hi, Kai," Jade murmured, batting her long eyelashes at him and making her friends giggle. Jade always went for athletic guys, so the girls were not surprised that she seemed to be crushing on their surfing instructor already.

Kai passed out surfboards to the girls – a pink one for Cloe, a turquoise one for Jade, an orange one for Sasha and a peach one for Yasmin, all of which totally coordinated with the girls' beach style.

"Do I look like a surfer yet?" Jade asked, striking a pose with her board.

"Absolutely!" Yasmin agreed.

"Yeah, now you just have to learn how to actually surf," Mya pointed out, sharing a smirk with Lani.

Unfazed by Lani's snotty comment, Jade said, "Eh, details, details."

"Well, why don't we start on some of those details?" Kai suggested, giving Jade a warm smile that made her blush.

Kai started by helping the girls figure out which foot should go in front on their boards, showing them how to wax their boards and fasten their leashes to their ankles to keep their boards from being swept away by the waves.

Next, they all stood watching the waves crashing on the shore, observing how they carried the surfers who were already out there. "Are you starting to get a sense of what these waves are up to?" Kai asked, and the girls nodded in agreement.

"Now, let's try paddling out into the water," he suggested. "You need to get a sense of balance on the board before you

can do anything else. Centre your body on the board with your legs straight out behind you, and paddle with your arms. Do you think you can do that?"

"Yep," Jade agreed before anyone else could answer, and hurried towards the water. She splashed into the waves and settled herself onto the board, paddling around in the shallow water of the beach's cove with her friends at her side.

"This is so much fun!" Cloe squealed.

"This is nothing – wait till you ride your first wave!" Kai declared. "It's the most amazing feeling in the world!"

"Whoa!" Yasmin cried, slipping off of her board with a splash.

"Yas, are you okay?" Sasha gasped, paddling over to her friend.

Yasmin shook wet strands of her golden hair out of her face, grinning. "Guess I need a little more practice, huh?"

Mya opened her mouth to make another of her snide comments, but Sasha pinned her with a glare so fierce that she shut her mouth again without saying a word. There was no way Sasha was letting someone kick her friend while she was down.

Instead, Mya turned to Cloe and declared, "Wow, you're a natural, girl!"

A huge smile spread across Cloe's face as she paddled even faster. "Who knows, maybe I'll be a surfing champion by the time I leave."

"I'd believe it," Lani agreed, while Cloe's friends exchanged annoyed looks behind her back. That girl was shamelessly buttering up their friend, and they really had to wonder what she was up to.

The girls continued paddling around until Kai finally told them their lesson was over for the day.

"But we didn't even get to ride a wave!" Jade protested.

"Don't worry, you'll get your chance," Kai assured her, leading the way back to the beach. "This was a great start for our first lesson, and we'll do even more next time!"

The girls carried their boards back to the sand, tilting their heads back to soak in the warm sunlight.

"I could get used to this," Yasmin sighed.

"Are you *sure* we don't have time to just lie on the beach for a while?" Cloe asked, gazing longingly at the expanse of glittering sand, dotted with umbrellas and brightly coloured beach towels.

"We have to get to Hawaiian history class," Sasha reminded her. "And Miss Lang's co-teaching it with Ms Sato, so she'll definitely notice if we skip out on it!"

Yasmin loved learning about history – as a writer, she saw it as a collection of amazing stories like the ones she liked to write herself. But she could tell that her friends were getting bored – they would rather try something themselves than hear about things other people did in the past.

"I can't believe the other girls got out of this session," Cloe muttered. She looked like she was missing her new friends already.

"Well, they've probably learned all this before," Yasmin pointed out. "And now it's our turn to find out."

"Did you know that the first Hawaiians actually came here from the islands of Marquesas?" Ms Sato asked. She clicked a button to show images of Marquesans in traditional garb on the projection screen.

"Followed by a wave of Tahitians 500 years later," Miss Lang added, clicking through a new set of photographs.

Yasmin leaned forward in her chair, fascinated, but next to her she caught Jade stifling a yawn.

"Which is why we thought you should learn a little bit about Marquesan and Tahitian culture while you're here, too," Ms Sato declared.

She flicked on the lights and swung open the classroom door, and in walked Mrs Kauwe, followed by Kaila and Alana in short yellow skirts and Mya and Lani in delicately fringed white dresses.

Yasmin's friends immediately perked up. "Wait, what's going on here?" Sasha asked.

"This trip is all about bringing history and culture to life," Miss Lang declared, "so we thought the best way to teach you about the original Hawaiians would be to show you."

"So these girls will be demonstrating traditional Marquesan and Tahitian dances, and then I'll teach you a few moves too," Mrs Kauwe declared.

"Awesome!" Jade squealed, her excitement propelling her out of her seat.

Mrs Kauwe pulled out her iPod and portable speakers and turned on a pretty

Marquesan song. Alana and Kaila took their places in the front of the room and began swaying from side to side in time to the music, weaving their arms above their heads and pivoting quickly so their skirts flared out around them as they whirled through their routine.

The dance was faster than the hula, and when it ended, the girls and their teachers all burst into spontaneous applause.

After the applause died down, their dance instructor turned on an upbeat Tahitian tune. Lani and Mya launched into a fast-moving dance with lots of twirling, swiveling and twisting, waving their arms in rhythm with their rapid turns.

This dance was even faster, and the audience was so swept up in the dancers' energy that they all exploded into cheers once it was over.

Lani and Mya gave the onlookers a quick bow, and then Cloe, Jade, Sasha and Yasmin hurried to the front of the room, eager to master these two new styles of dance as well. This was one history lesson they could all enjoy!

Chapter 6

That night, Sasha stood in the middle of their hotel room, shuffling through a few steps of hula then stopping, shaking her head, and starting again, clearly frustrated.

"How's that routine coming, Sash?" Cloe asked from her perch on the bed.

"Not so hot," Sasha admitted. "I'm usually totally immersed in a dance style before I try choreographing an entire routine, so right now I don't feel I have enough material to use."

"What about the dances we learned today?" Yasmin suggested, glancing up from her laptop, which she had set up on the suite's desk. "Can you use anything from those to help flesh out your routine?"

"I guess I could ..." Sasha began, looking thoughtful. But then she shook her head decisively. "No, I'm supposed to come up with a hula dance. What we learned today wasn't hula, so I can't really use it."

"Yeah, but the whole point of today's lesson was that those two cultures are part of the Hawaiian culture," Jade pointed out. She was stretched out on the couch, decompressing after another busy day, but she sat up to encourage her friend. "I think it would make your routine even better if you incorporated elements of all three dance styles."

"That *would* be pretty cool," Sasha admitted. "And it would definitely make my dance different from the ones that are already out there, and you know I love the chance to be totally unique!"

Energized by her friends' idea, Sasha

began stringing together a few different steps from each of the types of dance they had learned, and soon her friends jumped up and started following along with her.

"Okay, that could work," Sasha told them. "But to really put together a routine, I need the right music." She pulled her iPod out of her pocket and scrolled through until she found a fun song by a Hawaiian artist she had started listening to as soon as they began planning this trip. Popping it into her speaker dock, she told her friends, "Tell me what you think of this."

While they listened, Sasha ran through the steps she had just been practising, adjusting the sequence and timing to fit the rhythms of the song.

"Sasha, that was perfect!" Yasmin gushed once the song was over.

Sasha shook her head. "Not yet, it wasn't." But then a smile lit up her face and she added, "But it will be!" And her friends knew it was true.

Once Sasha's routine was on track, Yasmin returned her attention to the song she was trying to compose on her laptop.

"Ugh, you guys, I don't know what this song should be about!" she cried after staring at her computer screen for what felt like forever.

"Write about how amazing Hawaii is," Cloe told her.

"Yeah, I'm trying to," Yasmin replied. "But, I don't know, it just doesn't sound right."

57

©MGA

"Let's hear it," Jade said, but Yasmin looked horrified at the thought.

"No way! It's not even close to ready!" She closed her laptop firmly and strode away from the desk. "I think I just need some more practice time on the uke to help me get a better sense of the sound I need for this song."

"Well, for now we'd better get some rest," Sasha pointed out. "You know we have another long day tomorrow." Exhausted, her friends had to admit she was right.

Now that the girls had sampled lots of different aspects of Hawaiian culture, it was time for them to focus in on their ukulele playing for their big concert, and hula dancing for their big recital. And, of course, they needed to devote time to catching their first big wave.

The next morning, they arrived at Mrs Kauwe's dance studio while the pale pink and dreamy purple tendrils of sunrise still glowed on the horizon.

"I feel very lucky to have you girls with me all day today," their teacher announced. "We're going to have so much fun together!"

The girls smiled back at her, equally excited, but also nervous. They had all done a lot of dancing, but never a day-long workshop. Jade could have sworn her feet started to ache at the mere thought of dancing on them for that long.

But Sasha was pumped at the prospect of an all-day dance workshop. She loved to dance, and this full immersion was bound to help her improve her own routine.

Mrs Kauwe was determined that they would learn the basics of the routines they would

be performing the following week. "This first dance tells the story of how Hawaii came to be," she explained. "Watch the first time through, and then I'll start teaching you the steps."

She began demonstrating the dance with Alana, Kaila, Lani and Mya performing the same movements on either side of her while the other girls watched, fascinated.

"That was so beautiful," Yasmin sighed when they finished the routine. "Can you really teach us to do that?"

"That's questionable," Mya muttered under her breath so that their teacher wouldn't overhear her rude remark.

"Absolutely!" Mrs Kauwe declared. "You'll get it in no time."

The girls all removed their shoes and began following their teacher's lead, swaying gently

in imitation of the graceful motions of her arms and feet. And she was right – the movements felt so natural that they just flowed from one to the next, almost without having to think about it and, as Sasha knew, that was the way truly great dancing should be.

"This next one is about our love for the ocean," Mrs Kauwe continued once they were comfortable with the first routine. She performed the dance along with her helpers, and soon the girls all joined in as well.

"And our final routine is one about the last Hawaiian monarch, Queen Lili'uokalani," their teacher announced. This last dance was very upbeat and energetic, with lots of foot tapping and arm waving, skirt swishing and gazing joyfully up towards the sky.

"That was so much fun!" Jade squealed after they ran through their third routine. She was out

of breath from hours of dancing around, but she was having so much fun that she couldn't stop smiling and felt like she would burst from joy.

"Great work, girls," Mrs Kauwe said, beaming at all of her students. "In fact, I think you've earned a break."

But as the girls started to file outside, she pulled Jade, Sasha and Yasmin aside. Cloe noticed and tried to hang back too, but her teacher waved her away. "I just need to talk to these girls for a minute," she explained.

Cloe looked hurt at being left out, so Yasmin told her, "Great, we probably messed up. See you out there, Clo."

Cloe headed outside with her new friends, still looking unconvinced and upset to be seperated from her three best friends. She'd thought this trip would totally bond them closer together, but the opposite seemed to be true!

"Told you that you were a better dancer than the rest of them," Lani said to Cloe as they strolled through the door with Cloe still glancing over her shoulder at Sasha, Yasmin and Jade.

"Oh, I don't know ..." Cloe replied, but she smiled at the compliment.

"Is everything okay with you and Cloe?" their teacher asked once the door swung shut.

"She thinks we've forgotten her birthday," Sasha explained.

"And she's mad that we keep sneaking off without her," Yasmin added. "But we're just trying to plan an awesome surprise party for her!"

"Once she sees this wonderful luau you're planning for her, she'll cheer right up," Mrs Kauwe assured them. "And I had a great idea – what if we combined the recital with

Cloe's party? That way you won't be rushed trying to do both things on the same day, plus you'll be guaranteed amazing entertainment – yourselves!"

"That sounds perfect!" Jade exclaimed. "Do you think you can get Miss Akana to agree to let us do our concert at the luau too? That would be awesome."

"I'm sure I can," their instructor agreed.

"Thank you so much," Yasmin gushed. "This is going to make our lives so much easier!"

©MGA

"Always happy to help," Mrs Kauwe replied happily. "Now, go and enjoy the rest of your break, okay?"

The girls rushed outside, where Cloe, Lani and Mya were clustered together, chattering away, though they stopped talking as soon as Cloe's best friends joined them.

"So, are you in trouble?" Cloe asked in a cool, clipped voice.

"Nah, she just wanted to go over a couple of things with us," Jade told her, keeping her tone casual so Cloe wouldn't suspect anything was up.

"Glad to hear it," Cloe said before continuing her conversation with her new friends.

Her best friends knew she was just feeling hurt, and they couldn't wait to reveal their big birthday plans so things could get back to normal between them. They just hoped things wouldn't get too much worse before Cloe's birthday came around.

Chapter 7

Yasmin was facing some serious writer's block. After spending a full day practising the three songs they would be playing on the ukulele at the end of the following week, she had returned to her room eager to get to work on her original song. But the most she could manage was a few lines before she got completely stumped and found herself staring at her computer screen again.

Jade walked up behind her and tapped her friend on the shoulder, making Yasmin jump. "We're heading to a bonfire on the beach. Wanna come?"

"I don't know ... I really need to make some progress on this song," Yasmin replied sadly.

"Oh come on, I think you deserve a

break!" Sasha declared. "Besides, maybe inspiration will strike once we're out in the night air, relaxing on the sand, watching the flickering flames of the bonfire while the waves roll onto the shore."

"Wow, Sasha," Yasmin said with a smile. "That was totally poetic! Are you sure *you* don't want to write this song?"

"Nah, I'll leave it to you," Sasha told her. "But see, this place must be utterly inspiring if it can make even me sound like a writer!"

"Okay," Yasmin agreed. "I'm clearly not getting anything done here, so I might as well have some fun!"

Cloe was sprawled across the bed, her headphones blaring, and Jade had to wave her hands in front of her friend's face to get her attention. "Are you going to come to the bonfire too, Angel?"

Cloe yanked her earbuds out of her ear. "The bonfire? Oh, yeah, Lani and Mya asked me to meet them there."

"We're going over there now," Sasha added. "Why don't we all go together?"

"Oh, yeah, I guess that could work," Cloe agreed, though she sounded reluctant.

"What, don't you want to be seen with us?" Jade teased, though she suspected there was some truth to her words.

"No, it's just ... well, I promised I would hang out with Lani and Mya, and I get the sense that none of you like them very much." Cloe twisted her hair around her finger nervously, waiting to see how her friends would react to what she had said.

"Um, it seems to me like they're the ones who don't like *us*," Sasha replied.

"Okay, whatever," Cloe snapped. "But

you're the ones who are always avoiding them – and me." With that, she hopped off the bed and stalked out of the room before her friends could say another word.

"Well, I think that went well," Jade joked once the door had slammed behind their friend, trying to lighten the mood.

"Ugh, I wish we could just tell her about the party so everything could get back to normal," Yasmin sighed. "I hate having her mad at us!"

"But the surprise party will make her so happy," Sasha insisted. "Trust me, it'll be totally worth it."

"I hope you're right," Yasmin replied grimly, but she sounded unconvinced.

"See, this is why we need to live near the beach," Jade declared. She was stretched out on the cool sand with the heat of the bonfire warming her face. Their classmates were gathered around the fire, talking and roasting marshmallows.

"Anyone ready for a little campfire singing?" Lani asked, holding her ukulele.

"We're always up for singing!" Yasmin cried. She didn't even let it bother her when Lani shot her an annoyed look.

Lani began strumming a pretty version of "What a Wonderful World," and soon all the girls were harmonizing together.

"Wow, we sound great together!" Cloe exclaimed when the song was over.

"Yeah – maybe we should try doing things all together more often," Yasmin suggested quietly.

Just then, Kaila and Alana arrived and motioned their new friends off to the side.

"Here we go again," Cloe sighed, rolling her eyes.

"We'll be right back," Jade assured her, before hurrying along the beach to catch up with the other girls.

"I was at the store this afternoon, and I found some adorable hibiscus-print tablecloths we can use at the luau," Alana announced excitedly once they were far enough away from the fire that they couldn't be overheard.

"Ooh, and my grandma has a delicious punch recipe that we can make so we can have something tasty and tropical for everyone to drink," Kaila added.

"I was also thinking we could hold it at the Cultural Institute," Alana continued. "The courtyard there is really beautiful, and that way we'd be close to a kitchen and everything else we need."

"Man, I'm glad we have you girls helping us out!" Sasha exclaimed.

"And I talked to Ms Silva today, and she works with a florist all the time to get flowers for her leis, so she can get us a deal on pretty flower arrangements," Sasha told them. "Plus she offered to make leis for everyone!"

"That's great!" Yasmin declared. "All the teachers here are so cool!"

"Mr Jones agreed to dig an imu pit for us so we can have a traditional kahlua pig roast," Jade chimed in.

"Eww, you mean like a whole pig?" Yasmin gasped.

"That's what you have at a luau," Kaila explained with a shrug.

©MGA

"Well, if we have too ..." Yasmin said. "We are having other stuff too though, right?"

"Oh, yeah, there's always tons of food at a luau!" Alana assured her.

"Mr Jones said he would make laulau chicken, lomi salmon, sweet potatoes, rice and poi," Jade continued.

"What's poi?" Sasha wanted to know.

"It's a sort of a paste made out of taro," Kaila told them. "It's a staple food throughout Hawaii, like rice in other parts of the world."

"Most non-Hawaiians don't like it," Alana warned them. "But you should at least give it a try."

"I'll try anything once," Sasha declared.

"Ooh, you also need to try haupia," Alana added. "Mr Jones is making that too, right?"

"Sounds familiar," Jade said uncertainly. "What is it?"

"It's a coconut milk dessert, kind of like flan," Kaila explained. "It's yummy!"

"Mmm, this luau is sounding better and better," Jade announced. "I can't wait!"

"Me neither," Yasmin replied. "Because then we'll finally have our Cloe back!"

Her best friends had to admit that making up with Cloe would be the best part of all.

"So everything's all set then?" Sasha asked. She pulled out her BlackBerry and scrolled through her to-do list, the lighted screen glowing in the darkness.

"Yep – I think we've actually pulled it all together," Jade agreed.

"Except the entertainment," Yasmin pointed out. "I don't think we're ready at all!"

"But we will be," Sasha promised. "With everything else at this luau taken care of, we've got plenty of time."

"I hope you're right," Yasmin sighed, looking uncertain and worried.

The girls meandered back towards the fire, but when they arrived, the others didn't look at all happy to see them.

"Is your little secret meeting finished?" Cloe demanded, glaring at her friends.

"It's nothing secret — Kaila and Alana just wanted our advice," Jade informed her.

"If it's not secret, then why did you have to run away from us to talk about it?" Mya snapped.

"Because they were talking about *us*." Lani stared at them across the fire, her eyes flashing in the orange light of the flames.

"We weren't, I swear!" Yasmin cried, her voice high-pitched with distress.

"Uh-huh, that's what they all say," Mya replied with malice in her voice.

"You know what?" Cloe said, standing up and brushing the sand from her legs. "I think I've had enough of this bonfire for one night."

"Me too," Mya agreed, and Lani nodded.

"Cloe, why don't you sleep over at my place tonight, so your friends don't wake you whenever they decide to go home?" Lani suggested in a sickly sweet voice.

"Wait, I thought you were totally opposed to sleepovers," Jade reminded her.

"Yeah, well, Cloe's convinced me that they're a ton of fun," Lani told her. "*If* you have the right people there."

With that, Lani, Mya and Cloe strutted off down the beach, leaving the other five staring after them.

"Are you *sure* she'll forgive us once she sees the luau?" Yasmin asked worriedly. "She seems so mad she may not even show up!"

"Of course she will," Sasha assured her, but even she was starting to wonder if things were going too far.

Chapter 8

While her new friends gossiped and giggled, Cloe lay in her sleeping bag with a knot in her stomach. She felt just awful about feuding with her friends, but she reminded herself that they were the ones who had started it. They had forgotten her birthday, they had been abandoning her throughout this vacation, and it was only Lani and Mya who had kept her from being totally miserable over the past week on the exchange.

"I wish you could stay in Hawaii," Lani told her, interrupting her thoughts.

"It is really amazing here," Cloe admitted. "But I'm actually kind of eager to get back home to my normal life."

"But then you won't be able to hang out

with us anymore," Lani pointed out.

"Yeah, but maybe my friends will go back to being normal once we're home," Cloe replied sadly. "They've been acting totally weird since we got here."

"So, what do you care?" Mya asked. "If they want to ditch you, let them. You have way cooler friends now — us!"

"You don't understand," Cloe protested. "We've been best friends, like, forever. I've been through so much with those girls. And even though they aren't

©MGA

being so great right now, I know they'll come around sooner or later."

"That's sweet," Lani said, giving her a falsely sympathetic smile. "But don't you think some friendships aren't meant to last forever?"

"You mean like us and Kaila and Alana?" Mya suggested.

"Exactly," Lani agreed. "See, all four of us used to be best friends too, but after a while Mya and I realized that we just didn't really have that much in common with those two anymore."

"So we cut them loose!" Mya chimed in.

Cloe looked from one girl to the other, shaking her head. "I just don't think I could ever do that. Not to my very best friends."

Although she liked Lani and Mya, Cloe couldn't help wondering why they were trying so hard to talk her into giving up on her

friends. Suddenly she didn't feel like talking anymore.

"You know, I'm really beat. I should get some rest." She rolled over to face the wall, and while the other two continued to whisper, she wondered what her best friends were doing right then, and if they missed her as much as she missed them.

"I know how we can fix this," Yasmin declared, bouncing with excitement on the edge of her bed and waving her arms in the air.

"How?" Jade asked skeptically.

"We need to let Lani and Mya in on our party plans." Yasmin looked from Sasha to Jade, but was met only with blank stares from the two of them.

"Why would we ever do that?" Sasha wrinkled her nose in disgust at the very idea.

"Because then they can start helping us, instead of undermining us all the time," Yasmin explained.

"Yeah, but would they even be willing to do that?" Jade inquired. "Or would they give the whole surprise away just to mess with us?"

Yasmin pursed her lips thoughtfully. "I guess that's possible ... but I'd rather risk it than see Cloe so miserable for even one more day."

"But I'm not convinced that they would stop telling her mean things about us, even if they know what we're planning," Sasha said.

"I know, but it's the only thing we can do, short of just telling Cloe about the party," Yasmin insisted, "and I know we don't want to do *that*."

"You're right that we have to try something," Jade agreed. "I've never seen Cloe this upset."

The girls shared a smile at that – Cloe was a major drama queen, so they knew that anything that got her even more worked up than usual had to be a big deal.

"So we're agreed?" Yasmin asked. "We'll talk to them tomorrow?"

Jade and Sasha didn't say anything for a long moment, but finally Jade admitted, "I guess we don't have a choice."

Seeing how worried her friends looked, Yasmin gave them a smile. "Hey, this could work! And then everything will be okay again!"

"Yeah, it could work," Sasha muttered. "Or it could totally backfire …"

The next day, the girls were all waiting for their cooking class to start when Cloe slipped into the bathroom, and her friends took the opportunity to approach Lani and Mya.

"We need to talk," Sasha declared.

"What do *you* want?" Mya demanded, crossing her arms over her chest.

"Yeah, what are you doing?" Lani hissed.

"It's about Cloe," Yasmin continued.

"About how you've been totally dissing her all week?" Lani asked. "Or about how she likes us better than you, and you can't handle it?"

"Actually, no," Jade snapped. "See, here's the thing. We've been busy planning a surprise birthday party for Cloe, which is why we haven't been spending as much time as usual with her."

"Oh," Lani murmured. "That's really nice."

"And the only way we can make her feel better is to ruin the surprise," Yasmin added.

"Which is where you come in," Sasha explained. "Do you think you can keep her spirits up until the big day?"

"She's been pretty happy whenever she's around us," Mya informed them. "It's just you guys who are bumming her out."

"Quit it, Mya!" Lani cried. "They're trying to do something really nice here, and all we've been doing is badmouthing them. So I think we owe it them to help them out."

"Really, you're gonna help?" Yasmin gasped. "That'll make everything *so* much better, I just know it!"

Mya started to protest, but Lani clapped her hand over her friend's mouth. "We'd be glad to help. Really, it's the least we can do when you're going to so much effort for your friend."

That was when Cloe reappeared and gazed at them all suspiciously. "What's going on here?"

"Nothing!" Lani insisted. "We were just, you know, waiting for you."

"All right, girls, let's try out this recipe for chicken luau," Mr Jones said before Cloe could ask anything else.

"I want to go to a luau," Cloe muttered.

"Then we'll have to make sure you get a chance to while you're here," Lani declared.

"Really?" Cloe asked excitedly. "You would do that for me?" She shot a look at her best friends before turning her back on them again, obviously trying to make her point.

"Of course!" Lani agreed. "It's a fabulous Hawaiian tradition that you should all get to experience while you're here. There's food, and dancing, and music – it's a really good time, guaranteed."

"That sounds wonderful," Cloe sighed.

"Then we'll make it happen," Lani promised. "After all, we're supposed to be your hostesses while you're on the island!"

Cloe's friends were happy to see her perk up so much, but they couldn't help worrying that now Lani would get the credit for all their hard work and organisation.

While Cloe bent over her prep table, mixing the sauce for the chicken, Lani turned and winked at Cloe's best friends. They all smiled back at her, but still had to wonder whether she was really on their side now, or if this was another scheme to lure Cloe further away from them.

Chapter 9

Yasmin finally knew what her new song should be about. She rushed back to her room after class and began typing rapidly, the lyrics flowing effortlessly out of her. When she was finished, she read through the song, making a few small changes, but she was mostly very pleased with what she had written.

"What're you up to, Yas?" Jade asked, strolling into their room.

"Just writing an awesome song," Yasmin replied with a grin.

"Let's hear it!" Sasha cried, following Jade in.

"Well, I'm not totally sure about the melody yet – I need your help with that, Sasha – but here's what I'm thinking so far." Yasmin began to sing a song about friendships that last forever, no matter what, in her sweet, clear voice

She reached the end of the song, and her friends burst into applause. "That melody is great," Sasha told her. "I have some ideas to fill it out a little, but it's really beautiful as it is." She hurried to grab her ukulele so she could start trying out some harmonies and getting the tune pitch perfect.

"I wrote it for Cloe," Yasmin murmured.

"I know you did," Jade said, putting a comforting arm around her friend. "And she's going to love it. Once she hears that song, there's no way she can stay mad."

Sasha rushed back over to her friends and started strumming away on her ukulele. Soon Jade and Yasmin grabbed theirs and joined in, Yasmin singing her lyrics while her friends strummed along.

They were enjoying a full-out jam session when Cloe burst into the room.

Her friends stopped playing when they saw her, but she said, "Don't let me disturb you. I just need my sunglasses, and I'll be out of your way, don't worry."

"You aren't in our way!" Yasmin protested. "We were just rehearsing my new song."

"And I see you don't need any help from me," Cloe snapped. She snatched her sunglasses off the dresser and stalked out of the room, ignoring her friends' calls to stay.

"Well, I think we can say that things aren't better yet," Jade said once Cloe was gone.

©MGA

"No kidding," Yasmin muttered. She played a few notes on her ukulele, but they sounded as mournful as she felt.

"It'll be okay," Sasha promised. "We just have to wait it out for a few more days."

After a little more rehearsal, Jade, Sasha and Yasmin hurried over to the music room to play their song for Miss Akana.

"That's lovely, girls," she declared. "And it really makes use of the unique sound and feel that a ukulele provides!"

"I wanted to give it a real Hawaiian vibe, while still expressing my own musical style," Yasmin explained.

"Well, you did it!" their music teacher replied. Yasmin couldn't stop smiling at her teacher's compliments.

"We'll have to get everyone started on

this song right away," Miss Akana continued. "Can you girls write up sheet music for everyone to use?"

"No problem," Sasha agreed. "But we were hoping we could have some extra rehearsals just for this tune."

"I guess we could fit in some extra time," Miss Akana told her. "Any particular reason?"

"This song is part of our birthday present to Cloe," Yasmin explained. "We'd love to have your other students play it with us, but if Cloe's in on the practice sessions, it'll ruin the surprise."

Miss Akana raised her eyebrows. "Don't you think she'll notice if you're all off playing without her all the time?"

"Yeah, she will," Yasmin admitted, hanging her head. She felt like things with Cloe were doomed to get worse and worse.

"Ooh, but I know how we can fix it!" Sasha cried suddenly. She dashed towards the door, and with a shrug, her friends followed behind her.

"Where are we going?" Jade gasped, hurrying to keep up with her friend.

"You'll see!" Sasha shouted over her shoulder. She turned down the hallway and darted into the dance studio. She glanced around before spotting Mrs Kauwe sorting through piles of paper in her office just off the studio.

"Mrs Kauwe, we need your help!" Sasha exclaimed, hurrying into the office.

Mrs Kauwe glanced up from her papers, looking dazed. "Of course – what can I do for you girls?"

"Well, first, I wanted to show you the hula routine I came up with," Sasha began. Her friends stared at her, stunned.

"I don't know if we're ready for that," Yasmin pointed out. They hadn't practised their new dance since Sasha first came up with it, and they certainly weren't prepared to perform it for their teacher now.

"You'll be fine!" Sasha assured her, though Yasmin and Jade both still looked nervous. Mrs Kauwe followed them into the studio, where Sasha pulled her iPod out of her purse and popped it onto the teacher's speaker dock. She scanned through and found the song she had chosen for her dance and hit play, taking her place between her best friends, facing the wall of mirrors.

Sasha launched into her routine with her friends following her lead. She was right – it all came back to them once they got started, and soon they were all moving in synch, fluidly echoing the rhythm of the music that filled the studio.

"That was fantastic!" Mrs Kauwe declared as the group performed their last pose. "Sasha, did you really come up with that whole thing yourself?"

"But of course," Sasha replied proudly.

"I'd be honoured to debut your routine at our recital," their teacher said. "But what did you need from me?"

"I want Cloe to be the featured dancer in this routine," Sasha explained, "so I was hoping you could come up with some modifications to make her part really special, and also give her some private

©MGA

96

lessons so that she'll be totally amazing on the big night."

"Are you sure *you* don't want to be the lead dancer?" Mrs Kauwe asked, looking surprised at Sasha's generous offer.

Sasha nodded decisively. "Definitely. This would mean a lot to Cloe, and I know she'll do a fabulous job. Plus it will keep her busy while we practise the song Yasmin wrote for her."

Mrs Kauwe promised to coordinate with Miss Akana to make sure that Cloe's private lessons coincided with their secret song rehearsals and kept their secret safe.

Once their classmates began arriving for their dance class, Mrs Kauwe pulled Cloe aside. "Sasha just showed me the routine she choreographed, and I'd really like you to take the lead in performing it. You're an awesome dancer and you're totally tuned in to Hawaii"

"Really?" Cloe gasped, her voice brimming with excitement. But then she turned to Sasha and asked, "Sash, are you okay with that?"

Sasha smiled – those were the kindest words Cloe had spoken to her all week. "I would love it," Sasha assured her, and Cloe's smile grew even bigger.

"Now I'll need to schedule extra practice time with you," Mrs Kauwe continued. "Are you up for that? I know you girls are being kept super busy while you're here."

"Totally!" Cloe squealed.

The girls began practising the routines they had learned last time, with the addition of Sasha's dance at the end, and Cloe cheerfully whirled through the moves, looking happier than she had since they arrived in Hawaii.

Jade and Yasmin kept shooting Sasha

grateful looks as they danced, thrilled that her plan seemed to be paying off.

Chapter 10

"Now, I know you're busy preparing for your cultural performances," Miss Lang told them in their history class the next morning. "But don't forget, you also need to prepare a presentation on an aspect of Hawaiian culture which you'll be giving in front of your other teachers and me on your last morning here to show how much you have learned."

"Wait, I didn't know about that!" Cloe cried, distraught at being out of the loop.

"It was in the materials we got when we were accepted to the programme," Yasmin told her. "Didn't you read them?"

"I did, but I didn't commit every word to memory," Cloe snapped. "We can't all be as perfect as you, Yasmin."

Yasmin took a deep breath, fighting back the tears that brimmed in her eyes at her best friend's harsh words.

"So is it a group project, or what?" Cloe asked their teacher, pretending not to notice how hurt her friend looked.

"You can choose to give a ten-minute presentation on your own, or if you want to work with others, just multiply that by the number of people in your group," Ms Sato explained.

"What do you think, girls?" Jade asked. "Are you up for a 40-minute team presentation?"

"I'd rather work on my own," Cloe snapped before anyone else could answer.

"Okay, how about a half-hour presentation for the rest of us?" Sasha suggested, and Jade and Yasmin nodded.

As Miss Lang and Ms Sato began running through some suggestions for possible presentation topics, Yasmin slumped at her desk, too upset to listen closely and take careful notes as she usually did in her classes.

"Yasmin, are we boring you?" Miss Lang demanded.

Yasmin immediately sat up straight. "No, no, you were talking about how the Hawaiian language only has 12 letters in its whole alphabet, which is pretty cool. Do you think you could teach us a few words?"

"Of course," Ms Sato answered for her. "You already know 'aloha,' which can be a greeting or farewell, though it also means so much more than that. Another important

word to know is 'mahalo,' which means 'thank you,' but also signifies respect and admiration."

"It's cool that you can say so much with just one word," Jade said.

"It's a truly amazing language," Miss Lang agreed.

"Another word you'll hear a lot here is 'ohana,' which means family, but can also include close friends," Ms Sato continued, enjoying her students' enthusiasm.

"So I could say these girls are my ohana?" Sasha asked.

"Exactly," Ms Sato replied.

"That's awesome," Sasha declared, trying to catch Cloe's eye, to remind her that they really were a family to each other, but her friend avoided her gaze.

"How do you say 'I'm sorry' in Hawaiian?" Yasmin murmured.

"'Ua kaumaha au'," Ms Sate told her.

"Ua kaumaha au," Yasmin repeated, looking at Cloe, hoping her friend would respond. She thought she saw Cloe's stiff posture soften slightly, but Cloe still refused to look at her.

"I can't believe we have to put together a presentation on top of everything else we're supposed to be doing," Jade complained while lounging on the beach with her friends after their surfing lesson.

"Well, this trip *is* supposed to be educational," Yasmin pointed out.

"Hey, I'm learning plenty of things!" Jade protested. "But that doesn't mean I want to give some boring report on all the cool stuff I've learned."

"Then we'll just have to make sure it isn't boring," Yasmin told her.

"Do you guys have any idea what we should talk about?" Sasha asked.

"I was thinking since we're learning all about hula and music anyway, we could do it on the importance of music and dance in Hawaiian culture," Yasmin suggested.

"Love it!" Jade squealed. "We could probably even work in a song and dance to use up some of our time."

©MGA

"Great idea, Jade!" Yasmin cried. "In fact, I know exactly the song we could use – Aloha 'Oe!"

"Ooh, I love that song," Jade agreed. "But can we really do a whole presentation on it?"

"Absolutely!" Yasmin told her, sitting up on her beach towel in her excitement. "That song was written by Queen Lili'uokalani herself, and she used it as her official farewell to her people when Hawaii became part of the United States in 1959."

"Oh wow, so there's a ton of history we can talk about there!" Sasha exclaimed.

"So we'll learn the lyrics, and the dance that goes along with the song – although maybe someone should accompany us on ukulele, too," Yasmin continued.

"I'll do it," Jade cried. "I don't think I can handle another dance routine right now!"

"It's kinda hard to sing and dance at the same time," Sasha pointed out, "so Yas, why don't you sing, and I'll dance, and Jade will play?"

"Perfect!" Jade and Yasmin declared in unison.

"So we'll open with the song, and then explain the history behind it, and then get into how this is just one example of how music and hula are woven into the entire culture," Yasmin suggested, jotting down notes in the writer's notebook she always kept with her.

"Sounds good to me," Jade agreed, laying back on her beach towel and adjusting her sunglasses on her face. "And now that we've got that all planned out, I think we deserve a little break!"

Although they still had a ton of research

to do, not to mention party planning and any number of rehearsals, her friends stretched out on the sand beside her, eager to relax for just a little while.

Chapter 11

The final Saturday of their stay arrived faster than any of the girls would have thought possible, which meant it was time for Cloe's birthday luau, their presentation, a surfing showcase, and their recital, all in one day.

They had been practising like crazy, and they finally felt like everything was ready. Everyone had worked extra hard to learn Yasmin's song in time, even Lani and Mya, while Cloe had totally mastered the solo for Sasha's dance.

Jade, Yasmin and Sasha could hardly contain themselves – they were so eager to spring their big surprise on Cloe. But Cloe spent the morning stomping around their room, furious that all of her best friends had completely forgotten about her birthday.

"Should we wish her happy birthday?" Yasmin whispered to the others while Cloe was getting dressed in the next room.

"We can't!" Sasha protested. "It'll be a way bigger surprise if she thinks we completely forgot about her birthday."

Yasmin bit her lip nervously, but nodded her agreement.

That was when Lani and Mya rapped loudly on the door, and Yasmin let them in.

"Is Cloe almost ready?" Lani asked cheerfully, a sweet expression on her face.

"I'm sure she'll be out any minute," Jade replied, knowing how long Cloe could take to get ready to go out.

"Hey, once you're outside, could you make sure to wish her a happy birthday?" Yasmin whispered. "We haven't, because of the surprise party, but I think it would really cheer her up to hear it from someone."

"Of course," Lani agreed. "Aren't you glad all this secrecy will be over soon?"

"So glad," Yasmin sighed.

Cloe strode out of the bathroom and straight out the door, motioning to her new friends to follow her.

"We'd better get over there too," Sasha reminded them. She and her friends glanced in the mirror, adjusting their matching strapless dresses, which were the bright pink of tropical punch.

"We look good," Jade declared. "And

©MGA

just think – it's only our first cute outfit of the day!" She was totally thrilled at the prospect of that day's costume changes. They would all be wearing swimsuits for their surfing demonstration, followed by coral-coloured halter dresses for their recital, before changing into cute outfits of their own for the rest of Cloe's party.

"Ready, girls?" Sasha asked.

"Always!" Jade and Yasmin replied, hurrying out the door with their ukuleles and costume changes in hand.

"So I guess Yasmin never did finish her song, huh?" Cloe asked her new friends with a smirk over at the classroom where they would be making their presentations.

"I guess not," Lani replied reluctantly.

"And it's a good thing Mrs Kauwe decided to save Sasha's routine by having me take the lead," Cloe continued. It felt good to rant about her friends when they had treated her so badly. Ignoring her and avoiding her were bad enough, but completely forgetting her birthday was the final straw.

"Your solo is awesome, but Sasha did come up with a pretty cool dance on her own," Lani protested.

"Yeah, right," Cloe scoffed, assuming her friend was being sarcastic, but she fell silent as their teachers entered the room, followed by the other five girls.

"All right, we have a lot to do today, so let's get started," Miss Lang announced once everyone was seated. "Who wants to go first with their presentation?"

Cloe's hand shot up into the air. "I will."

She hurried to the front of the room. "I'm going to be talking about the aloha spirit,"

she began. "It's the spirit with which we were welcomed to these islands, the spirit of warmth and sincerity that infuses every aspect of life here." She smiled at Lani and Mya. "It means treating others with mutual respect and building relationships on an equal basis." She paused to give her friends a pointed glance. "But did you know that the aloha spirit is officially on the law books here in Hawaii? The Aloha Spirit Law encourages even the governor, legislature and judges to do their jobs with this spirit in mind."

When she finished her speech, everyone applauded. "Are there any questions?" Cloe asked, scanning the faces before her.

Yasmin raised her hand, and Cloe gave her a curt nod. "I was just wondering if the aloha spirit would include thinking the best of others, even if you're upset with them."

"I guess so," Cloe agreed begrudgingly.

"Then I'm a big fan of the aloha spirit," Yasmin declared as Cloe sat back down, her face flushed bright pink.

Then it was Jade, Sasha and Yasmin's turn to present. At the front of the room, Jade began strumming her ukulele, Yasmin started singing and Sasha glided into her dance.

Everyone clapped again after the song, and then the girls shared the song's history. "Hula has been around for centuries, and it traditionally involves both dance and chanting," Jade explained.

"The ukulele only became popular in Hawaii a little over a hundred years ago, but now it's one of the most commonly recognized symbols of Hawaii," Sasha added.

When they finished talking, the room filled with thunderous applause. "Girls, you did an incredible job of weaving together history and performance!" Miss Lang cried.

Cloe glowered at her friends, wishing she had joined in on their presentation instead of trying to manage all by herself.

"I thought Cloe's was pretty cool too," Yasmin interjected, garnering a small smile from her friend.

"Definitely," Miss Lang agreed. "I'm so proud of you girls! You've all learned so much since we've been on this island."

"Let's just hope we've learned how to surf!" Jade muttered. They had been so focused on their dancing and singing that practising their surfing had definitely ended up at the bottom of their priority list.

The girls changed into swimsuits and sarongs in the centre's locker room and headed for Waikiki along with their teachers. Kai met them on the sand, along with their surfboards.

"All right girls, ready to catch a wave?" he asked with a grin.

Jade, Sasha and Cloe had all managed to ride a few waves at their last lesson, but Yasmin had barely managed to stay on her board, so she was especially nervous.

But they all paddled out into the ocean, waiting for the perfect wave. "I'm going for it!" Jade shouted as she watched a wave swell. She turned to face the shore and let the wave carry her forward, hopping onto her feet at exactly the right moment. "Woohoo!" she squealed as she rode the wave all the way to the shore, feeling like she was flying through the air.

After watching her, her friends felt ready to try it themselves. Sasha and Yasmin both went for the same wave, coasting to the shore side by side, laughing as they surged along. Finally Cloe took her turn, and they all watched from the sand as she balanced on her board, an expression of pure joy on her face as she approached them.

"Looks like I taught you all well!" Kai exclaimed.

"Great surfing, girls," Alana agreed.

"Whew, I can't believe we made it!" Yasmin gasped.

"Now we just have to get through our recital," Sasha reminded her.

But first, they had to set up everything for Cloe's luau. Lani and Mya whisked Cloe away for lunch, while everyone else worked on decorating the centre's courtyard. Sasha laid out the tablecloths and set the tables while Jade strung paper lanterns from the trees. Kaila whipped up her grandma's punch and Alana set up tiki torches and arranged bouquets on each table.

Mr Jones prepared the cooking pit and started roasting the pig, then dashed into the kitchen to fix all the side dishes with Yasmin's help.

Mrs Kauwe and Miss Akana set up speakers and a small stage at the far end of the courtyard, and Ms Silva strung orchid leis with Kai's help.

"They're coming!" Alana called, spotting Cloe and the others on their way inside.

"Places, everyone!" Sasha cried.

They all crowded by the entrance to the courtyard, and when Cloe strolled in, they shouted, "Happy Birthday, Cloe!"

Cloe froze, completely overwhelmed. "Wha – what's going on here?"

"We're throwing a birthday luau for our best friend," Yasmin explained, stepping forward and giving her friend a hug.

"You guys did all this?" Cloe gasped.

"Well, we had some help," Jade admitted, gesturing to their teachers and new friends.

"But I thought you'd all forgotten my birthday," Cloe said, tears glistening in the corners of her eyes as she broke into a huge smile.

"That's what we wanted you to think," Sasha told her. "It was the only way we could make this party a total surprise!"

"Wow," Cloe murmured. "You girls are the best! I'm so sorry I ever doubted you."

"And we're sorry we gave you reason to," Yasmin added. "I hope you agree that it was worth it!"

"Totally," Cloe agreed. "I'm just sorry I was so mean to you this whole time!"

"And I'm sorry we got off to such a bad start," Mya added. "You girls turned out to be totally cool."

"I'm just glad we're all friends now," Jade replied. Looking at Kaila and Alana, she continued, "We *are* all friends, right?"

"For sure," Lani said, turning to her old friends. "Working with you girls on this party and the song and everything reminded me of how much fun we used to have together. I'm really hoping we can be friends again."

"I'd like that," Kaila murmured, while Alana nodded her agreement.

While they all chattered happily, Ms Silva draped a lei around each girl's neck. "No luau is complete without them!" she declared as the girls admired the gorgeous blooms.

"We have another surprise for you," Yasmin told Cloe. She and the other girls, now decked out in their coral sundresses, pulled out their ukuleles and jumped on stage. "This is a song I wrote called 'Ho'aloha,' or 'friend', and it's dedicated to my best friend Cloe."

"Awww!" Cloe squealed from the audience, as the seven other girls began to sing and play. At the end of the song, Cloe rushed onstage and pulled them all into a hug. "That was so amazing!" she gushed. "That's my new favourite song!"

©MGA

They performed the rest of their songs, then started their hula routines, which all went great too – especially Sasha's original dance, with Cloe taking the lead.

"Dinner is served!" Mr Jones announced, carrying platters full of food out of the kitchen. They all grabbed food and punch before taking their places around the picnic tables.

"Mmm, did I mention how much I love Hawaii?" Jade asked, biting into a delicious piece of sweet potato.

"Did I mention how much I love you girls?" Cloe chimed in.

"Did *I* mention how glad I am that we're all friends again?" Yasmin added.

"Here, here!" Sasha cried, holding up her punch glass, and all eight of them, old friends and new, shared a toast and a giggle while the gentle strains of Miss Akana's ukulele playing, the sweet scents of Ms Silva's

flowers, the rich aroma of Mr Jones' cooking, and the cool breeze of a perfect Hawaiian evening all floated over them.

"This really is paradise," Cloe sighed, and her friends all nodded – they couldn't have agreed with her more!

Read more about Bratz in these other awesome books!